How to
Trick a Tiger

Richard Brown

Illustrated by Rowan Barnes-Murphy

CAMBRIDGE
UNIVERSITY PRESS

Cambridge Reading

General Editors
Richard Brown and Kate Ruttle

Consultant Editor
Jean Glasberg

PUBLISHED BY THE PRESS SYNDICATE OF THE UNIVERSITY OF CAMBRIDGE
The Pitt Building, Trumpington Street, Cambridge CB2 1RP, United Kingdom

CAMBRIDGE UNIVERSITY PRESS
The Edinburgh Building, Cambridge CB2 2RU, United Kingdom
40 West 20th Street, New York, NY 10011-4211, USA
10 Stamford Road, Oakleigh, Melbourne 3166, Australia

First published 1998

Printed in the United Kingdom by the University Press, Cambridge

Typeset in Concorde

A catalogue record for this book is available from the British Library

ISBN 0 521 63570 5 paperback

**Other Cambridge Reading books
you may enjoy**

The Best Present Ever
Sally Grindley

A Walk with Granny
Nigel Gray

Carnival
Grace Hallworth

**Other books by Richard Brown
you may enjoy**

Rachel's Mysterious Drawings

The Midnight Party

ONE

The sun beat down at the edge of the
forest. Tiger and Jackal woke from a doze.

"I'm getting very hungry," Tiger growled.

"So am I," said Jackal. "We haven't eaten
for two days."

"VERY hungry," Tiger growled again,
louder this time.

Jackal trembled. When Tiger was hungry, he was bad-tempered, and when he was bad-tempered, he got very fierce. You never knew what he might do next – or what he might eat.

They came out of the trees and into a half-ploughed field.

"Look!" said Jackal, his eyes lighting up, his stubby tail wagging.

"Ah, now *that* looks tasty," said Tiger, licking his lips.

In the field was a farmer ploughing with an ox. A rather scrawny ox, as it turned out, but still tasty enough to make a good tiger-breakfast!

"Stay here," Tiger commanded. "If you're lucky, you might get some bones to gnaw today."

Tiger padded silently across the field and up behind the farmer. He sat down, bared his sharp, gleaming teeth, and roared.

The farmer – whose name was Manu – thought thunder had clapped just above

his head. When he turned and saw Tiger's sharp, gleaming teeth, he nearly fell flat on his back with fright. The ox's legs trembled too, as if the earth was shaking beneath him.

"Stand aside, Farmer. I want my breakfast."

"Br-br-br-breakfast?"

"The ox, you dolt! There's not enough flesh on *you* to satisfy a jackal."

Manu was so relieved that *he* wasn't on the menu, that he began to smile nervously.

Then a terrible thought struck him. Glancing at his trembling ox, he said, "But that's the only ox I've got. If you eat him, I shall be forced to pull the plough myself. It'll break my back!"

"Tough!" said Tiger. "Now move aside."

"No, wait!" cried Manu. His head was in such a spin that he hardly knew what he was saying. "I've got a better idea."

Tiger looked at the farmer suspiciously and said, "It'd better be a *good* idea. I'm VERY hungry, you know. I'm not in the mood to wait."

Sweat stood out in beads on Manu's brow. And then he had an inspiration! "If you could bring yourself to wait a *little* longer . . ."

Tiger growled. He raised his paw and spread his sharp, curved claws.

"Yes, you see," stammered Manu, "at home my wife's got a nice, fat milking cow. It'd be much more tasty and tender than my scrawny old ox."

Tiger lowered his paw. "Tasty, you say? Tender? Fat?"

"Yes," gasped Manu eagerly. "She's fat with milk and laziness, I promise you. Let me go home and fetch her."

Tiger examined his claws. The thought of the cow made his mouth water so much he began to dribble. And the ox did look rather tough and scrawny. "Go on, then," he said. "But if you're gone for too long, I shall eat the ox anyway."

With that, Manu hurried home to his wife. His knees knocked together so much that he kept stumbling as he ran.

TWO

Sati, Manu's wife, had just finished milking her cow when her husband appeared.

"Manu?" she said, surprised to see him home so early. "What are you doing here? Get back to your field!" She was always bossing her husband about, but he was so used to it that he hardly noticed it any more.

"Sati," he said, gasping for breath. "There's a tiger in our field and it's about to eat my ox."

But instead of being frightened, Sati laughed! She was amused to see how terrified her husband was. "That'll mean you'll have to plough the field yourself, won't it?" she said. She went on stroking the flank of her cow, pretending that as far as she was concerned, the tiger had nothing to do with her.

Manu looked at her in amazement. "No, you don't understand. I've promised the tiger your cow instead."

15

Sati froze; her eyes were daggers. "You've done what?" she said through gritted teeth. "Oh, you stupid fool!"

Manu wrung his hands. "And we haven't got much time. You've got to let me take her."

But Sati wasn't having that! "So, you think you can just come and take my precious cow, eh?" she said in disgust. "Typically selfish! I suppose you couldn't have thought of another way of getting rid of him?"

Manu looked shamefaced. "Me? What can *I* do against a tiger?"

Sati shook her head in despair. "What a husband! All right, now listen. Go back to the tiger and tell him that I'll bring along the cow in a minute or two, as soon as I'm suitably dressed."

Manu's face changed. "You mean it?"

"Don't I always mean what I say?"

"Of course. But he won't mind what you're wearing. Can't you come now?"

"No! I'll come when I'm ready!

Manu wrung his hands again. He didn't fancy going back to the tiger empty-handed. But he had no choice. He turned and, with slow steps, he made his way back to the tiger, wondering what Sati was up to.

When Tiger saw him coming across the field without the juicy cow, he was furious. "What?" he roared. "I've got to wait even longer?" He lashed his tail and bared his teeth.

"My w-w-wife is br-br-bringing the cow," Manu stuttered. "She'll be here in a m-m-minute, I'm sure."

"She'd better be," Tiger growled. He prowled around the trembling man and the trembling ox, his mouth watering, his whiskers quivering.

Suddenly he heard the pounding of hooves. He pricked up his ears fearfully. The pounding came closer and closer. And then a fierce-looking prince on horseback came riding into the field. A shiver went up Tiger's back.

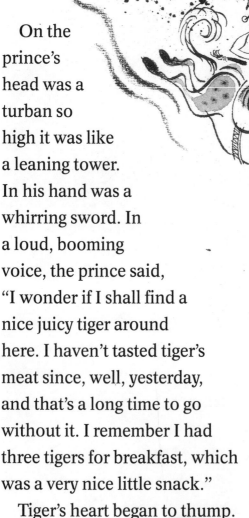

On the
prince's
head was a
turban so
high it was like
a leaning tower.
In his hand was a
whirring sword. In
a loud, booming
voice, the prince said,
"I wonder if I shall find a
nice juicy tiger around
here. I haven't tasted tiger's
meat since, well, yesterday,
and that's a long time to go
without it. I remember I had
three tigers for breakfast, which
was a very nice little snack."

Tiger's heart began to thump.
Not just a prince, but a tiger-eating
prince! That huge turban, that
sword . . .

He began to back off.

"Aha!" cried the prince. "Is this a tiger
I see before me?" He spurred on his pony
and galloped across the field, straight
at Tiger.

Down went Tiger's tail. The
thunder of the hooves, the
towering turban, the whirring
sword . . . Everything
frightened him.

He fled back across
the field with terror
in his heart.

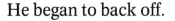

The prince came to a halt beside Manu.

Manu began to bow. "Your majesty," he said, "I'm so grateful . . ."

The prince laughed aloud and said, "It's me, you dolt."

"You? Who? Oh!" A look of amazement crossed his face. "Sati! It's you! But I thought . . ."

"I think I make rather a good prince, don't you, with my tall turban and rusty sword."

Her laugh echoed across the field.

THREE

Tiger hid beneath the leaves at the edge of the forest, his sides heaving, his great tongue lolling out. "That was a close one," he gasped, listening to the fearsome prince's laugh.

Jackal trotted up. "Whatever's the matter, my lord?"

"Why didn't you warn me?" Tiger
growled. "You must have known there was
a tiger-eating prince living around here."

"Prince? Around here? Are you sure?"
Jackal looked startled. He peered through
the leaves into the field. Then he laughed.
"Oh, but you can't mean that farmer's wife,
dressed up to *look* like a prince, can you?"

"Farmer's wife? What are you talking
about?"

"Her, out there. Look, can't you see her pigtail hanging down behind the turban?"

But Tiger refused to believe he'd been tricked. "That's NOT a farmer's wife, I tell you. That's a terrifying, tiger-hunting prince. Look at his sword. Look at his terrible, burning eyes . . ."

"Huh! You're scared!" Jackal jeered.

"I'm NOT," roared Tiger.

But Jackal was delighted. "Scared of a farmer's wife!" he shouted, dancing around in glee. "Just wait until I tell everyone in the forest that Tiger ran away from a farmer's wife."

Tiger swished his tail furiously now. "You knew this was going to happen, didn't you?" he hissed.

"Me? Of course not. How could I?"

"You knew a prince lived around here. And the prince paid you to bring me here, didn't he? He bribed you!"

"Are you serious?"

Tiger got up and loomed over Jackal. "Whose idea was it to come here anyway? It wasn't mine."

Jackal felt Tiger's hot breath on his neck and his laughter died in his throat. "If you don't believe me," he said, "let's go back together and take a closer look at this so-called prince. *Then* you'll see that the prince is really the farmer's wife."

But Tiger was by now *very* suspicious. "Oh, yes," he said, "and you think I'll fall for that one too? As soon as we get near the prince, you'll turn tail and run. What do you take me for?"

Jackal didn't like being accused of this, even by Tiger. He had his pride. "Well," he

said, "if you still don't believe me, then let's tie our tails together. I won't be able to run away then, will I? *Then* you'll see I'm right."

Grudgingly, Tiger agreed. They tied their tails together with a tight reef-knot. Then they set off back through the forest to the field.

Manu and Sati were still in the field, laughing over the joke they had played on the cowardly tiger. But when Manu saw Tiger return, with a jackal tied to his tail, he went very white and his teeth began to rattle. "Look! We are lost! They've guessed who you really are. They'll eat us all up now."

"Don't be a fool," said Sati coolly. She shielded her eyes and watched the animals approach. "Just leave this to me."

When Tiger and Jackal were within earshot, Sati raised her voice and boomed across the field, "Ah, Mr Jackal. How kind of you to bring me a nice fat tiger for my breakfast. As soon as I've eaten my fill, you can have the bones, *just as I promised you*."

Tiger stopped in his tracks, making Jackal stumble over in the dust. "I knew it! You tricked me!" he hissed through his trembling whiskers.

"I didn't," Jackal protested.

Sati advanced towards them, waving her rusty sword.

In a panic, Tiger turned tail and fled across the field, bumping poor Jackal over the furrows, bump-bump-bump, as he went. "Is he gaining on us?" Tiger gasped as they neared the trees. But Jackal was too bruised and winded to answer.

Sati let out a great whoop of triumph, and then she slid off her pony and collapsed in a heap of laughter.

Tiger and Jackal crashed into the forest. With panic in every step and leap, Tiger dragged Jackal through briars and ditches. Sati's terrrifying cry echoed in his head. They did not stop until they were full of scratches and covered with bruises, far away from the farmer's field.

It took them until night time to undo the knot in their tails.

As soon as he was free, Jackal crept away, reflecting that at times it did not pay to be too clever. Nor was it wise to make friends with a coward.

Tiger went to sleep feeling very hungry. He dreamed he was being chased by a horde of princes in tall turbans, each with a pigtail flying behind him.

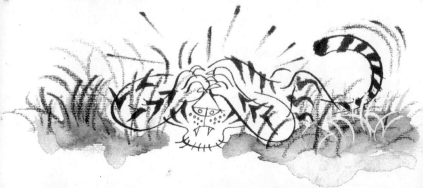